THE WEDDING OF
THE RAT FAMILY

THE WEDDING OF
THE RAT FAMILY

retold by Carol Kendall
illustrated by James Watts

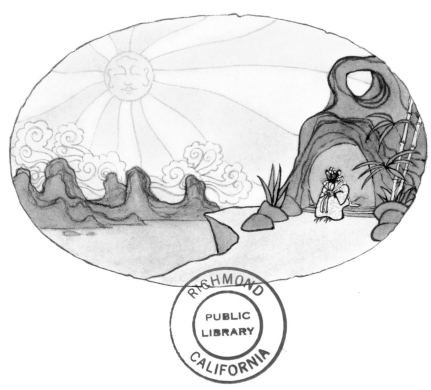

Margaret K. McElderry Book
NEW YORK

*Especially for
Ming-hui (Julia) Lin,
who started it all....*
C.K.

For Mom, with love

Copyright © 1988 by Carol Kendall
Illustrations copyright © 1988 by James Watts

Margaret K. McElderry Books
Macmillan Publishing Company
866 Third Avenue
New York, NY 10022
Collier Macmillan Canada, Inc.

First Edition

10   9   8   7   6   5   4   3   2   1

Composition by Linoprint Composition Co., Inc., New York, New York
Printed and bound by Toppan Printing Company in Japan

Library of Congress Cataloging-in-Publication Data

Kendall, Carol.
*The wedding of the rat family / retold by Carol Kendall ;
illustrated by James Watts.—1st ed.*
p.   cm.
*Summary: Aspiring to a marriage of power and influence for their
daughter rat, two rat parents arrange a calamitous wedding with a
member of the cat family.*
ISBN 0-689-50450-0
[1. Folklore—China.]   I. Watts, James, ill.   II. Title.
PZ8.1.K359We   1988
398.2'45293233'0—dc19   88-2197   CIP   AC

Long years ago in China, in a moldy dark cave near the
Yellow River, there dwelt an uncommonly proud rat
family. Such a lofty bearing and mincing gait as they

displayed were sadly at odds, however, with those occasions when—too often!—they had to scrounge in kitchen dumps for their dinner or, even worse, scuttle for safety on all fours. It was not a glorious life being a rat, whether proud or humble, in that countryside. If plagues of locusts didn't nabble the grain out of the nearby fields, the Yellow River rose in flood and drowned it out; and if there was enough grain to store after such catastrophes, fire swept the granaries before the rats had gnawed proper holes through the wall. At home, if the cave wasn't tail-deep in flood water, there was always the terror of polecats and stoats lurking just beyond the doorsill, ready to snatch rat children at the twitch of a whisker.

In spite of calamity and catastrophe, however, the high-nosed rat wife and her husband held themselves well above the ordinary run of rodents living in neighboring caves. In the matter of ancestry, as they often reminded these rats of lesser station, *their* family dynasty could account for ten-thousand times the ancestors of the Emperor and Empress of China put together. Truly, were rats to follow royal custom and build burial mounds for their own dear departed ones, the face of China would be nothing but humps and bumps marking the last resting place of illustrious rodents.

Indeed, according to the rat wife, her ten-times-great-grandparents had dined at kings' tables, as she put it, although in truth they had dined *under*, rather than *at*, the royal board, and *after*, rather than *with*, kings. Fact or fancy, it was all the same to their humble cousins, Dusty Answer and Nimble Nail, who listened to these tales with jaws agape in admiration and trained their myriad daughters and sons to kowtow with proper reverence to their highborn relatives.

In due course, the highborn rats' youngest daughter
came of age, and it was time to think of marriage. Dusty
Answer and Nimble Nail had timorously mentioned their
numerous sons as possible suitors, but this suggestion was
so ridiculous that the illustrious rats stared their skin-and-
bone cousins right off the doorsill.

"With my noble ancestors," the father rat cried out to his
wife, "it is unthinkable that we continue to live in terror
and squalor in this musty cave! We must marry our
daughter Mulan *up* in the world! Power and Influence!
That's what matters—Power and Influence!" He beat on
the table with a feeble fist. "Why else name her after a
famous woman warrior, which, I believe was *your* ridic—
that is, *your* idea . . . my Precious!"

"And why not!" his Precious answered, showing sharp
teeth. "It's little enough glory comes to a wife, no matter
how wellborn—and may I remind you that my grandmother refused to gnaw in the same grain barn as your
grandmother! It is up to you to find a husband fit to be the
bridegroom of our own brave Mulan! . . . My Beloved," she
added with a dangerous smile.

"Yes, Precious," said her Beloved, "whatever you say becomes my command." His breath hissed between his teeth. "And just whom do you suggest I call on concerning this delicate matter? Will you make a list?"

"Naturally, I have already done so...my Beloved." Precious pulled a scrap of cloth from the grand teapot that had lost its spout and straightened it on the table. On it was printed in elegant lettering:

> To Be Eligible for Marrying into the Illustrious Rodent Dynasty of the Yellow River Caves, the Prospective Bridegroom Must Be:
> 1. Rich
> 2. Powerful
> 3. Influential
> 4. Of Ancient Ancestry

"Oh, excellent, excellent!" cried Beloved Rat. "A very comprehensive list, most cleverly thought out. But—I almost hesitate to suggest—do you suppose we might add another item? I'm thinking of, perhaps, 'Number 5. Quick as a Flash.' For you must agree that in this world it is woe to the slow. 'Woe to the slow,'" he repeated, pleased with

the effect. He prided himself on being something of a poet. "Or, 'Quick as a Flick'? That carries an air of certainty, don't you think?"

"Don't maunder. Quickness has nothing to do with what I have in mind."

"But my Precious, as we are at the top of the heap ourselves, how are we to find our equals, there being none equal to us...my Precious?"

Precious's patience was running thin. "Stop looking at your miserable feet," she bridled, "and look *up*. Whose light shines upon the world and everything in it? That all living things depend on?"

Beloved twitched his tail nervously. "You can't mean the *Sun*?"

"Exactly. Oh, yes, exactly...my Beloved."

Sprucing himself with generous sprinklings of rose dust, well rubbed in behind the ears, Beloved Rat set out that very night to address the most powerful personage in the world on behalf of their daughter's future happiness. It was a long, weary journey to the highest peak of the land, and he arrived just as dawn was breaking.

Busy as he was at waking up the world, the Sun listened most politely to Beloved's proposal before giving him a modest answer. "Good Mr. Rat," he said, "I understand your need, but in all honesty I must decline your good offices, for I am not, as you think, the most powerful being in the world. Black Cloud is stronger than I. Don't you know that Black Cloud can cover me from sight for days on end? Go call on Black Cloud."

Fearful of his wife's scorn, Beloved decided against going home to report the Sun's words. Instead, he went directly to seek Black Cloud, whom he finally found curled up in a hollow on a hillside.

But Black Cloud only laughed ruefully at Beloved's proposal. "Powerful? I? Not so, Master Rat. Listen a-while. I can be nigh bursting to give the land the good soaking of rain it craves when, *HOO-HOO!* along comes Wind and blows me out to sea, where there is already plenty of water." He looked quite bleak at the thought. "Go see Wind, if it's power you're looking for!"

His tail beginning to drag from weariness, Beloved sought out Wind, who was sulking in a valley and in no mood for propositions of any sort. "Whut! Whut! Whut!" he blustered, furious at being disturbed. "I've only just now come from bashing myself against Wall, and you show up with your pretty speeches about power and influence! *HOO-HOO!* Go tell your tale to Wall while I recover from my bruises. Wall is the bridegroom for your daughter!"

By this time Beloved was footsore and slack-jawed, but he drove himself on. At last he approached Wall, who looked at him so stonily that Beloved thought it were better to face his Precious in defeat than to put the question to this monstrous blank face.

However, there he was, and ask he must.

For answer, a stone rattled out of Wall, and Beloved had to jump out of the way. "Have a care!" he squeaked.

"*You* have a care," said Wall rudely. "It's rats like you that make me tumble down, you with your constant nibbling and gnawing at my crevices. Would I take a rat daughter in marriage? I would not! She would be the death of me!" Another stone jounced on the ground, almost depriving Beloved of his tail.

And so, at the end of the long, long day, Beloved dragged himself back to the damp cave and his Precious to admit the defeat of their plans.

"However, I have learned much," he said quickly, in an attempt to regain face. "Sun is blotted out by Black Cloud, Black Cloud is blown away by Wind, Wind is stopped by Wall, and Wall—listen to this, my Precious—Wall is brought to earth by none other than Rat! Our Mulan can marry her own kind and be proud of her bridegroom's strength! For we seem to be more powerful than all of these!"

"Of course," Precious said, her ears a-twitch with scorn. "I must just remember that the next time the cat pounces— while I am running for dear life."

"Oh. Yes. Yes.... I hadn't thought of that. The cat is indeed.... Hold! Did you say 'cat'? The cat family?" Beloved's eyes glowed red with sudden excitement, and his weariness fell away from him. "Oh, my Precious, my Life, you have given me a most wonderful idea!"

"Indeed."

"In*deed*, indeed! What is it that we dread the most? What is our most powerful enemy? Our most influential foe? Oh, perfection!" He gave a leap of joy. "Tails, long and sinuous! Eyes, crafty slits! Ears, sharp enough to hear dew forming! And whiskers? Splendidly twitching!" He drew himself up to make a mock salute. "My Precious, we must make our alliance with the cat family! Our daughter shall marry a cat!"

He was so overcome with his cleverness that he danced about the cave on his hind legs, waving his forelegs over his head in an excess of joy, until neighbors came rushing to see what the fuss was about. Precious watched her husband's unseemly cavorting with a deep frown, but soon her doubts were swept away by his enthusiasm, and, smiling so widely that her teeth glittered in the lamplight, she fell to writing up lists of friends and relatives worthy of being included in a wedding procession that would carry their daughter to a husband of such distinction.

A go-between was sent to the cat family to arrange the marriage. He came back to report that the cat family were well pleased with the prospect of enfolding the rat family into their own lives. Their very tails and whiskers had twitched in anticipation of such an event. Let it be an

occasion of great splendor, they had said, with two hundred and fifty in the wedding procession. They wanted no bone-thin sunken-cheeked rodents, either, for this was to be a gala occasion and called for jolly, plump attendants to make the day ring with sounds of merriment and feasting.

Precious and Beloved joyfully began gathering together a suitably grand dowry of rare seeds and beans, the best salt-rotted fish, web-stitched silks and satins, banners and scrolls, finely carved chairs and chests, and lanterns enough to light a hundred wedding processions. Twenty-six dressmakers fashioned the bride's wedding gown; seventy-three jewelers cut and polished precious stones to twinkle and wink round her head and ears, and eighty-two lesser artisans decorated her gown with brilliants of many colors.

Dusty Answer and Nimble Nail, elated at their illustrious cousins' good fortune, set to work with their myriad daughters and sons at constructing and contriving and decorating such furniture as sedan chairs and fine chests and fancy drums and gala banners. Never was furniture more beautifully crafted or embroidery more exquisitely stitched.

Both Dusty Answer and Nimble Nail, narrow-bodied rats to begin with, became more and more drawn out and sunken in as they labored mightily to finish the wondrous furniture for the wedding. As for the myriad children, their growth was quite stunted from too much work and too little food, but gladly they toiled on for the sake of their grand relatives. They measured and hammered and awled, they sewed fine seams and wove bright silk threads into patterns of long life and happiness, and they took no note of the empty rumblings of their stomachs as each day wore into night and night gave way to dawn.

It would be wrong to say that the two hundred and fifty rats chosen for the wedding procession were any less busy. Ten times a day they brushed clean their bodies from whisker to tail until each glossy hair stood alone. They cleaned their ears and their toes morning and evening, oftener if the ground turned muddy or the wind was full of dust. They ate twenty-four times a day, with snacks betweentimes, and afterward reclined motionless on their beds to let the fat settle around their bones. They gave up frisking about in favor of walking sedately on two legs, thereby not only presenting a noble appearance but running no danger of jostling away their new layers of flesh. If the cat family wanted plump rats, declared Beloved, then plump rats they should have!

The appointed day finally dawned, with Nimble Nail finishing her fine embroidery on the sedan chair even as the rat daughter was being helped into it, ready to be carried to her exalted bridegroom's house. The myriad sons and daughters were scattered amongst the other furnishings of the wedding, adding finishing touches under Dusty Answer's direction. There would scarcely be time to get themselves dressed and ready to join the procession, but such was their loyalty that they could not be turned from their work until it was finished and finished right.

And, oh, alas, when the procession finally moved off— with Precious and Beloved sitting fatly in their sedan chairs, and their daughter sitting plumply in her sedan

chair, and all the two hundred and fifty attendants walking with their corpulent stomachs before them—Dusty Answer and Nimble Nail and their myriad work-stunted children were still paint-smeared, needle-pricked, and worn away to shadows, no fit part of the gala procession demanded by the mighty cat family.

They were, in fact, too exhausted to weep over their loss, staying awake just long enough to see the triumphal procession take to the road that ended at the magnificent mansion of the cat family. Then they fell asleep on the spot, ere the sound of drums and flutes, fifes and gongs and cymbals, short trumpets and long trumpets had quite faded in the distance.

Before the procession reached the cat family mansion, there were far more than two hundred and fifty rodents in attendance. Twice that number had come from around the district to walk alongside the procession, eager to be part of such a grand occasion. They were thick and thin, long-tailed and short-tailed and cut-off-tailed, brilliant-eyed and dull-eyed, pert-eared and droop-eared, sleek and ruffled, all of them basking in the glory that was the rat family's.

Some of the bolder ones even managed to edge through the gate at the cats' mansion along with the wedding procession before the gates clanged shut, and that was a sad thing to happen to rats who only wanted to watch what was going on. For as soon as the plump wedding party was secured inside the walled courtyard of the mansion, the cat groom and all his relatives sprang upon the rat family and all *their* relatives—and ate them.

When news of the catastrophe trickled back to the moldy cave, Dusty Answer and Nimble Nail and their myriad daughters and sons were stricken with grief.

"As nearest kin, I must write a memorial," said Dusty Answer.

"Do as you must," said Nimble Nail. "*My* memorial will be to clear the mold out of this cave." And she put the myriad sons and daughters to sweeping and dusting and scouring and clearing the cave of its clutter. When that was done, she set them to gnawing and scratching at the walls until the rooms were large enough to accommodate the expected gathering for the reading of Dusty Answer's memorial.

The reading was a grand success, attended by all the remaining rats of the Yellow River Caves. There were refreshments aplenty, brought in from field and forest, and so many toasts drunk to the dear, departed ones that everybody became quite cheerful. It was voted unanimously to hold a memorial service each month of the year, with Dusty Answer and Nimble Nail in charge.

And so it came about.

Although the remaining rats were a puny lot to begin with, all the robust rodents having gone to the wedding, they soon picked up and became fat and happy.

Dusty Answer grew expert at writing memorials and was often in demand for public speaking of all kinds. Nimble Nail, of a more practical turn of mind, continued to enlarge the cave, adding new rooms and parlors and baths, and these she portioned out to rats of no fixed abode in return for supplies and services.

In proper rodent fashion, the myriad daughters and sons all found husbands and wives with whom to start families of their own. They never forgot the fate of those who aspired to a marriage of Power and Influence, but they saw nothing wrong in choosing the best, the strongest, the

cleverest, the most industrious rats for mates. It was only the sensible rodent thing to do.

Nothing in the rats' outer world had changed—floods, locusts, fire, stalking cats—but in spite of endless frights and alarms, the new clan of the Yellow River Caves flourished and again grew so numerous that their burrows and tunnels made lively humps and bumps across the face of China. Rodents had no need of ancestral mounds or of marryings into Power and Influence. For, as Dusty Answer was fond of putting forth in his speeches, couldn't they make Wall tremble and shake and finally bring him to the ground? Wall, who was stronger than Wind, who in turn blew away Black Cloud, the very same Black Cloud who dared to cover Sun himself?

What greater power could any rat ask?